Magic
Animal Friends

23

For Elizabeth Singh. With love

Special thanks to Conrad Mason

ORCHARD BOOKS

First published in Great Britain in 2017 by The Watts Publishing Group

1 3 5 7 9 10 8 6 4 2

Text copyright © Working Partners Ltd 2017
Illustrations copyright © Working Partners Ltd 2017
Series created by Working Partners Ltd

A CIP catalogue record for this book is available from the British Library.

ISBN 978 1 40834 412 5

Printed in Great Britain

The paper and board used in this book are made from wood from responsible sources

Orchard Books
An imprint of Hachette Children's Group
Part of The Watts Publishing Group Limited
Carmelite House, 50 Victoria Embankment, London EC4Y 0DZ

An Hachette UK Company
www.hachette.co.uk
www.hachettechildrens.co.uk

Charlotte Waggytail
Learns a Lesson

Daisy Meadows

ORCHARD

Brighteyes' Home

Spelltop School

Treehouse

Picnic Area

Twinkling Inkwell

Honey Tree

Sunshine Meadow

Map of Friendship Forest

Library

Playground

Greenhouse

School Hall

Madame Doodleflap's House

Can you keep a secret? I thought you could!

Then I'll tell you about an enchanted wood.

It lies through the door in the old oak tree,

Let's go there now - just follow me!

We'll find adventure that never ends,

And meet the Magic Animal Friends!

Love,
Goldie the Cat

Contents

CHAPTER ONE

A Wonderful Woodland School

"These pups are so adorable!" exclaimed

Jess Forester. She and her best friend, Lily

Hart, were in Lily's back garden. The

autumn sunshine was warm on their

backs. They were sitting in a wooden pen,

playing with three tiny, golden puppies

with flappy ears and curly tails.

"Someone handed them in to Helping Paw this morning," said Lily.

Lily's parents were vets, and they ran the Helping Paw Wildlife Hospital from a converted barn at the bottom of their garden. Lily and Jess spent every minute they could caring for the animal patients.

Jess scooped up the smallest puppy and giggled as it nibbled her blonde hair. It

 10

felt warm and soft in her arms. "They're unusual," she said. "What breed are they?"

"I'm not sure." Lily opened a book that lay at her feet. "I asked Mum and Dad, but they don't know either, so I got this book about dog breeds from the library."

Jess put her pup gently on the grass and bent over the book. "These puppies have squashy black noses like pugs but their ears are floppier." The pup pulled at her trainer laces. "Hey, don't do that, you cheeky thing!" Lily said with a giggle.

Jess picked up a rubber bone. "Play with this instead."

She rolled the bone across the pen. To her surprise, a paw poked out from under a blanket and batted the toy back.

A cat with gleaming golden fur crawled out from the blanket. She stretched and gave a friendly miaow.

"Goldie!" cried Lily.

"She's come to take us to Friendship Forest!" said Jess, beaming.

Friendship Forest was a magical land where the animals lived in wonderful woodland houses – and best of all, they could talk! Lily and Jess loved to go to their secret world with Goldie.

Goldie sprang out of the pen. Lily and Jess stepped out after her and shut the dogs safely inside.

"We'll be back before you know it," said Lily, blowing the puppies a kiss. No time passed in the human world while the girls were visiting Friendship Forest.

Goldie scampered out of the garden and across the stepping stones of Brightley Stream.

They followed her to the old, dead-looking tree in the middle of Brightley Meadow. As she got near, the tree sprang into life. Every branch shimmered with

 13

red, gold and brown leaves. Shiny green acorns popped up and squirrels chased around the trunk. Sweet singing filled the air as greenfinches swooped and dived in the dappled sunbeams.

Goldie touched the trunk with her paw and writing appeared on the bark. Giving

each other an excited smile, Lily and Jess held hands and read the words aloud.

"Friendship Forest!"

A door appeared in the trunk. Jess turned the handle. As the door opened, a warm yellow light flooded out. They tingled as they stepped through, which they knew meant they were shrinking, just a little. Then the warm light faded and they were in a clearing of blossom-covered trees that smelled of strawberries and cream.

Goldie was now standing on her back legs and wearing a glittery scarf around

 15

her neck. She was nearly as tall as the girls' shoulders, and they hardly had to bend to give her a happy hug.

"I'm so glad you could come," she told them. "Today's the first day of term at Spelltop School. Would you like to help the new little pupils settle in?"

"Yes please!" cried Lily, her dark hair swishing in excitement.

"We've never seen the school before!" said Jess, delighted.

Goldie led them through the forest, down a path lined with periwinkles and cheerful primroses.

Soon they came to a sign painted with shimmering stars in all the colours of the rainbow.

"Spelltop School," read Lily. "Wow! We're here!"

The girls gazed at the pretty thatched building with pink-and-white roses climbing up the walls. It stood on one side of a playground full of toys, climbing frames and hopscotch squares. Opposite was a cheerful yellow building with fairytale pictures on the walls and a roof that looked like a big open book. Alphabet bricks above the door spelled out "Welcome to our library".

Lots of young animals were hurrying

towards the school building, all carrying

bright backpacks and book

bags.

A little puppy with a pink flask on a strap around her neck ran up to them. "Hello, Goldie," she said, bobbing with excitement, before turning to the girls. "And you must be Jess and Lily! I've

heard so much about you."

Goldie smiled and said, "This is Charlotte Waggytail. It's her first day at school."

"You must be very excited," said Jess.

"I am," said Charlotte. "I can't wait to read all the books and learn interesting things. I am a bit nervous, though."

"You'll be all right, Charlotte," said Lily. "School is great! And we're coming today as well!"

Just then, there a sound of breaking branches came from behind them. The girls turned to see an orb of yellow-green light floating through the air, knocking back trees as it went. It came down to land just in front of them and they could see a woman standing inside, hands on her hips.

"Oh no," breathed Jess. "It's Grizelda."

The orb exploded in a cloud of stinky sparks and in its place stood a horrible witch. She wore a purple tunic and a black cloak that flapped behind her with a sharp crackling sound. Her green hair hung in lank, greasy tangles. The young pupils huddled together in fright.

Grizelda wanted complete control of

the magic forest. Lily and Jess had helped

their animal friends stop her evil plans

many times before, but she never gave up.

"We mustn't let her near the school!"

cried Goldie.

CHAPTER TWO

Grizelda's Evil Plan

Goldie and the girls leapt forwards into Grizelda's path.

"Quickly, little ones," called a calm voice. "Come inside where it's safe."

A large white goose wearing a black mortarboard was beckoning from a door.

"Go to Professor Gogglewing,

 23

children!" Goldie called, and the pupils rushed over to him. "Professor Gogglewing is the headmaster of Spelltop School," she explained. "He'll protect all the students."

Lily, Jess and Goldie stood firmly in front of the scowling witch.

"We won't let you harm the animals at

Spelltop School," said Lily firmly.

"I'm not interested in those silly little creatures," Grizelda cackled. She waved a dirty drawstring bag in their faces. "This is my witchy book bag," she told them. "I'm going to fill it up with all the books from the school library. Then I'll turn their magic from good to bad." She threw back her head and gave a nasty cackle. "With all those evil spells at my command, it'll be easy to take over Friendship Forest."

She swept towards the library, screeching with laughter.

 25

Lily and Jess raced after Grizelda, but before they could reach her, Charlotte the puppy darted forward and grabbed Grizelda's cloak in her front paws.

"You're not going to touch the books in my new school," she cried.

"Charlotte, be careful!" Jess cried.

Grizelda tried to pull her cloak free from Charlotte's paws. "Let me go!" She fixed Goldie and the girls with an evil glare. "And as for you three, don't come any closer or I'll turn this pestering pup into a potted plant."

Suddenly, the door to the library

opened and a strange creature came
hurrying out. He looked a bit like a green
caterpillar, with a pair of big, round
glasses. He was carrying a silver book
covered in sequins in his white-gloved
hands. He came up to the girls' knees –
until he reared up to face the witch.

"Professor Wiggly will know what to
do," said Goldie. "He's a bookworm – and

 27

the school librarian."

The professor opened the silver book and read out loud.

"Magic, shut our library door.

Make sure that's how it stays.

Keep our books all safe inside,

Far from her witchy ways."

As he spoke the words of the spell, shimmering silvery letters floated out of the book. They drifted towards the library,

where they melted into the walls.

"None of your spells will stop me!" shrieked Grizelda.

She wrenched her cloak free from Charlotte's grasp and stalked up to the library. But before she could get close, there was a loud bang and she was thrown through the air. She landed on her bottom, her green hair covering her face.

Lily, Jess and Goldie burst into giggles. Charlotte joined in.

"That will keep the books safe from your meddlesome magic, Grizelda," said Professor Wiggly. "And now I have some important reading to do." He scurried back into the library and closed the door.

"Now go back to your tower and leave Friendship Forest alone," said Jess.

"I'm not finished yet," screeched Grizelda, stumbling to her feet. "I've just thought of a wonderful, wicked plan. It's so clever, not even you pesky girls will be able to stop me!"

She shrieked with delight and vanished in a shower of disgusting, smelly sparks.

Lily and Jess looked at each other in horror. What was Grizelda up to – and would they be able to stop her?

CHAPTER THREE

Lily and Jess Lend a Hand

Professor Gogglewing came waddling over, flapping his wings in greeting.

"Thank you, Lily and Jess," he said. "Thank you, Goldie. You helped stop Grizelda for us."

"It was really thanks to Professor

Wiggly and Charlotte," said Jess. "Charlotte stood up to Grizelda."

The headmaster beamed at the little dog. "Welcome to Spelltop School, Charlotte!" he said. "Thank you for being so brave."

"I couldn't let that horrid witch take your books," said Charlotte. "I love reading so much that I'm going to read

every book in Spelltop School Library.
And now they'll all be safe because of the
library spell."

"They will indeed," Professor
Gogglewing assured her. "Although
Sycamore Class needs a book called
Perfect Plant Potions for their first lesson.
It has to go to the greenhouse – and it
won't be protected while it's out of the
library." He looked anxiously towards the
trees where Grizelda had disappeared.

"I'm going to be in Sycamore Class,"
said Charlotte. "I'll take it. I won't let that
nasty witch get her horrible hands on it."

She gave a fierce little growl.

"We'll go with you," said Lily. Goldie and Jess nodded in agreement.

The headmaster smiled. "Thank you," he said. "That would be so kind."

Charlotte scampered off into the library, her tail wagging furiously. The girls and Goldie followed her inside and gazed around the bright room. There were shelves laden with books of all shapes and sizes. Armchairs and big beanbags covered in soft velvet were placed under the windows, catching the sunbeams. They looked so warm and cosy that Lily

and Jess had to stop themselves grabbing
a book and curling up on them!

Professor Wiggly got up from his desk
and beamed at them all. "Welcome to
the library. Goldie, it's lovely to see you
again."

Goldie introduced him to Lily, Jess

 35

and Charlotte. The little puppy was still silently staring all around the room, her chocolate-brown eyes shining with delight.

"So, you're the plucky pup who stopped Grizelda in her tracks," said Professor Wiggly, smiling kindly at her. "You helped save our books."

"I had to," exclaimed Charlotte. "Books are so important."

"Professor Gogglewing asked us to fetch the book *Perfect Plant Potions* for

Sycamore Class," said Goldie.

"I'll get it for you," said Professor Wiggly. He picked up a long golden bookmark from his desk and waved it in circles like a wand.

The girls gasped with delight as a book on the top shelf gave a shiver and floated down into Charlotte's outstretched paws.

The girls admired the glittery green cover decorated with golden flowers.

"*Perfect Plant Potions*," said Lily,

reading the title. She gasped in surprise.

"*Written by Professor Wiggly.*"

"Professor Wiggly wrote most of the books in this library," said Goldie. "He's very clever."

Professor Wiggly's face went pink.

A tinkly bell sounded outside.

Lily and Jess ran to the door. The bluebell on the school roof was swinging merrily, sending out a delightful tune.

"The school bell," said Professor Wiggly.

"It's time for the first lesson to begin!" said Goldie.

Lily, Jess and Charlotte followed Goldie down a winding path of shiny coloured stones. They came to a big glass building among the trees. As they stepped inside the greenhouse, Lily and Jess breathed in

the wonderful scents from the rosemary and orange blossom plants that stood by the entrance. Sycamore Class were sitting on tall stools at a long table. The little animals chattered in excitement when they saw Lily and Jess. Molly Twinkletail gave them a happy wave.

A whiteboard had the words "Welcome, Professor Poppycud" written on it, but there was no sign of any grown-up.

"Professor Poppycud is going to be our teacher," Charlotte explained, carefully placing the potion book on the table. "I can't wait to meet her! My mummy said she's new to the school, just like us."

Just then the door opened and a
beautiful white cat trotted in. She had
deep blue eyes, long white fur – the

fluffiest Lily and
Jess had ever
seen – and a big
pink ribbon tied
in a bow on her
head.

"Hello, class,"
she said with
a large smile
that showed her

shining white teeth. Her voice was sweet, like chocolate cake. "I'm pleased to ..." She suddenly tripped on a pencil case one of the pupils must have dropped. She fell and knocked over the whiteboard. The little animals gasped in dismay as the whiteboard fell on to a shelf of plants. The shelf tipped up, sending the plant pots crashing to the floor.

"Oh no!" cried Charlotte. "Are you OK?"

Lily and Jess worried that the cat would be cross, but instead she shook herself, and started laughing. The pupils laughed along with her too.

"I suppose this is your teacher," said
Goldie with a chuckle.

CHAPTER FOUR

A Sneaky Spell

Lily and Jess helped the poor cat to her feet while Goldie and Charlotte cleared up the mess.

"Oh, wailing whiskers," said the cat, shaking leaves from her fur. "I'm sorry I made such a silly-billy entrance."

"We're just glad you didn't hurt

 45

yourself," said Jess.

"Thank you," said the cat. "Now I must introduce myself to everyone." She beamed at the class. "I'm Professor Cutiepaws. I'm here because Professor Poppycud couldn't come today. Poor dear thing."

She walked to the teacher's desk. "Let's make a start!"

Charlotte picked up *Perfect Plant Potions* and gave it to the new teacher. "Professor Gogglewing told me to bring this for the first lesson," she explained.

"Purrrfect!" said Professor Cutiepaws,

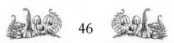

stroking the golden flowers on the glittery cover. "We'll have such a fun, fun, fun lesson."

The little animals looked at each other, their eyes shining, as their teacher began to flick through the pages.

"Which potion shall we make today?" she murmured. She tapped a page with her paw, her whiskers twitching in delight. "I've got the very one. The Faster Flower

Grower. This will make flowers bloom faster." She peered round at everyone, a happy smile on her face. "It's just the thing for super special days like parties and birthdays."

"Hurrah!" cried the class.

"Get yourselves into groups of four," beamed Professor Cutiepaws, "while I put the ingredients on the board."

Charlotte turned to Lily, Jess and Goldie. "Will you be in my group?" she asked shyly.

"We'd love to," said Lily. Jess and Goldie nodded enthusiastically.

 48

Professor Cutiepaws was making a list on the whiteboard in lovely curly writing. "Now gather all these wonderful things," she said, "and mix them up in a jug."

Everyone scampered off to the shelves at the end of the greenhouse to find their ingredients and jugs.

"I've found the hazel leaves and tulip petals," said Lily, her eyes running along the labelled jars on the top shelf.

"And I've got the silver bark shavings and ginger root," said Charlotte.

"I'll fetch the seven walnut shells of rainwater," said Goldie. She carried the

jug to a shiny water barrel in the corner.

Professor Cutiepaws walked round
helping. Suddenly she tripped over a stool
leg and crashed into the barrel. The water
sloshed out in huge splashes. "Oops," cried
the teacher as she slipped in a puddle and
knocked over a jar of pansy seeds.

"I'm such a butterpaws!" she exclaimed.

The class chuckled.

"Put your
ingredients in your jug and
give them a good stir!" said
Professor Cutiepaws.

She handed them all a tiny
perfect rose in a pink pot. "Now,
class," she said, "pour your potions
on to your plants. Carefully! We want
you all to be super duper
safe."

Each group picked up their jug and
poured. The roses gave a little quiver
and began to grow.

 51

"Our potions!" squealed Charlotte.

The roses were growing bigger and bigger. But then they started to change. The bright green stems were turning brown and brittle, and the flowers withered then transformed into spiky thorns.

"This can't be right," gasped Molly Twinkletail the mouse.

The animals cried out in dismay as long vines shot from the stems and wound themselves round the tables and chairs. Soon the whiteboard was smothered in dark, slimy leaves and the shelves were a tangle of waving roots.

 52

"How horrible!" squeaked Emily
Prickleback the hedgehog.

"Look out, everyone!"
warned Jess.

Vines were creeping
over the floor, twisting
and writhing between
the terrified animals.
Lily and Jess gathered
everyone together to
protect them. Jess could
feel the vines round her ankles.

"We must escape!" cried Goldie. She
bounded to the door and opened it.

Lily quickly ushered everyone outside.

Jess kicked away the vines at her

feet, snatched up the potion book and

stumbled to the door. But horrible weeds

were bursting out of the book. "Oh no!"

she gasped, trying in vain to pull them

away. "I can't stop them."

"There's only one person who could be

doing this," said Lily. "Grizelda."

"But how?" asked Jess, looking worried.

"Grizelda's nowhere to be seen!"

CHAPTER FIVE

Find the Twinkling Inkwell

Professor Gogglewing came waddling

out of the school. He raised his wings

in alarm when he spotted the nasty

vines bursting out of the greenhouse. He

beckoned quickly to the frightened pupils.

"Come into the hall, everyone. We'll be

perfectly safe there."

The little animals obeyed, their eyes round with fear.

"I'll find help to stop these horrible plants growing in our lovely forest," cried Professor Cutiepaws, rushing off into the trees.

Jess was struggling to hold *Perfect Plant Potions* as more nasty shoots sprouted from the pages.

"There's something very wrong with this book," said Lily, running to help her friend.

"We should ask Professor Wiggly about it," said Charlotte.

"That's a good idea, Charlotte," said Goldie. "He did write it, after all."

They dashed to the library.

Professor Wiggly looked up from a parchment scroll he was reading.

 57

"Whatever's happened?" he cried in dismay as Lily and Jess put the book on his desk. Weeds instantly grew from the inside and waggled like grasping hands.

"Everything went wrong when we tried to make the Faster Flower Grower potion," explained Charlotte.

The librarian pushed aside the slimy leaves and opened the book. "Oh dear, oh dear!" he exclaimed. "Grizelda must have changed this potion ... and the next one. You should never mix tulip petals and sticky buds, or apple pips and fuzzy moss." He checked all the pages. "In fact,

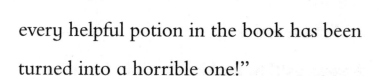

every helpful potion in the book has been turned into a horrible one!"

"But how did she do that when she can't get into the library?" asked Lily.

"I don't know," said Professor Wriggly. "But for now I'll have to write the spells out again and make them good spells once more. That will make everything go

back to normal."

Lily and Jess looked at each other in
relief and smiled.

Professor Wiggly
rushed to his desk and
opened a drawer. To the girls'
amazement, a crystal ink bottle
with a silvery top floated out and
settled on the table. A quill pen
made from a soft blue feather
followed, fluttering down to lie
neatly beside the ink bottle.

"Do you write the books with these?"
asked Lily.

Professor Wiggly nodded, beaming.
"They're magical," he told her. "Watch."

He sat down at his desk. At once, the
top of the ink bottle began to unscrew all
by itself. Then the quill rose up, feather
pointing in the air, and dipped its nib
into the bottle. But as it came out again,
Lily and Jess could see that there was
something wrong. There was no ink on
the nib.

"Oh dear," said Professor Wiggly. "The
magic ink has run out. I can't write the
spells again without it." He rubbed his
hands anxiously together. "Normally

Charlotte Waggytail

I'd go and fetch some more but I daren't leave the library in case Grizelda manages to break my spell and get inside. I must guard the books."

"We'll do it," said Lily and Jess together. Goldie stood beside them – she'd go too.

"I'm afraid it won't be easy," said Professor Wiggly. "The magic ink only comes from one place – the Twinkling Inkwell."

"Where's that?" asked Lily.

"Follow the trail of ink blots through the forest," explained Professor Wiggly. "They're flowers that look like puddles of blue ink. I hope you can find them among the weeds."

"We will," said Jess. "And we'll be back as soon as we can."

Charlotte put her chin up. "I'll come," she said bravely.

She led the way out of the library.

"Oh no!" she cried, pointing a wobbly paw towards the forest.

A terrible sight met their eyes. The spiky weeds had spread from the greenhouse into the trees around the school. Thick, grasping vines were slithering about like snakes, coiling themselves round the trees

and strangling the forest.

"The bad potion is spreading," said Goldie. "We have to hurry or we'll never be able to find the inkblot flowers."

They peered hard through the nasty creepers round their feet.

"Look!" Charlotte suddenly pointed at the forest floor. Just ahead lay something that looked like a big drop of beautiful deep blue ink. "An inkblot flower!"

The petals were all different sizes to make a puddle shape on top of a short blue stalk.

"Well done," said Goldie. "Now all we have to do is follow the trail."

"Kwark! Kwark!" A sharp sound overhead made them all look up.

Flying round the trees were four strange pink birds with sharp pointed beaks and spindly red legs.

"They're baby flamingos!" cried Lily.

"I've never seen flamingos here before," said Goldie in surprise.

"That's because we're new in Friendship Forest!" squawked the biggest bird. He landed on a high branch and began to preen his feathers with his beak. "I'm Gonzo, and I'm great."

"Never mind him," called the second flamingo. "Watch me! I'm Bingo, and I'm brilliant!" He swung round and round a branch with one claw, did a double somersault and flew down to land neatly next to Gonzo.

The third bird
swooped down beside
them with such a loud
screech that the girls
clapped their hands over their ears. "I'm
Banjo, and I'm the best!"

"I'm Cosmo," squawked the fourth
flamingo, "and I'm ...!" He
flapped in a dizzy circle,
then tumbled through
the air, nearly
knocking the
others off
their perch.

"He's clumsy!" said Gonzo crossly.

"Can you help us, please?" Charlotte called up to the birds. "We're searching for inkblot flowers. You might be able to spot them from up there."

To her surprise the four young flamingos began to laugh. "Ak! Ak! Ak!" They clapped their wings together and jumped up and down on their long, spindly legs.

"We're not going to help you!" Banjo screeched loudly.

"We're already helping someone else," squawked Bingo, doing the splits on the

branch.

Lily and Jess were worried. They guessed what the flamingos were about to say.

"Grizelda!" they all squawked together.

CHAPTER SIX

Trouble at the Inkwell

Goldie, Charlotte and the girls looked at each other in horror.

"Grizelda's going to destroy the forest," shrieked Banjo.

"Not if we can help it!" Charlotte barked back.

 71

"Ak! Ak! Ak!" laughed the birds.

"Let's go!" Jess whispered to her friends. "They're too busy laughing to see where we're heading."

The girls, Goldie and Charlotte hurried off through the forest. But the flamingos came after them. They could hear clumsy Cosmo crashing into the vines as he flew. The birds chortled when they saw Goldie's tail get caught round a spiky

weed and Lily catch her leg on a vine.

"We'll follow you everywhere!"
screeched Banjo.

Jess called her friends to a halt. "We'll
never get away from them like this," she
whispered. "Let's go underneath the vines
instead."

"Good idea!" Lily whispered back.
"Then they won't be able to spot us."

They dropped to their tummies and

slid along through the undergrowth. The
vines felt cold and slimy but they kept
going. Up in the trees they could hear the
flamingos' cross squawking.

"Kwark! I can't see them," shrieked
Bingo.

"We must find them," screeched Cosmo.
"Grizelda will be very cross if we don't."

The sound of flapping wings faded
away. Goldie risked a peek through the
thick leaves. "Your idea worked, Jess," she
said.

"We must find the well before they
come back," said Lily.

Charlotte poked her nose through the bushes. "Here's another inkblot flower," she called back. "And another."

As they followed the trail, they passed lots of the animals' woodland homes. Every door and window was covered in creepers and vines. Frightened eyes peeped out between the leaves.

"Don't worry," Goldie called to each family. "We're going to stop this spell."

At last they came to a clearing. In the middle stood a lovely well made from stones of different sizes. Its roof was covered in bright feathery quills. Under the roof, a silver bucket hung on a rope. There was a shiny handle fixed to a beam, to lower and raise the bucket.

"The Twinkling Inkwell!" gasped Jess. "We've found it."

"Hooray," cried Charlotte, wagging her tail in excitement.

Lily began to turn the handle. The

bucket disappeared
slowly into the
darkness.

Everyone listened.

Splash!

"Here comes the ink!"
said Lily. She turned
the handle to pull up the
bucket.

"KWARK!" One of the
young flamingos crashed
into the trees above,
sending down a shower
of leaves.

"Found you!" he squawked.

"Oh, no!" cried Charlotte. "It's Cosmo."

"Go away!" shouted Goldie.

"Shan't," squawked the flamingo, straightening out his feathers. "If you think you're getting the ink you're wrong!" He tumbled off the roof of the well.

Before the girls, Goldie and Charlotte could stop him, he opened his beak wide and bit the rope in half.

There was a horrible silence and then they all heard the bucket splash into the ink, deep down in the well.

CHAPTER SEVEN

Charlotte to the Rescue

Cosmo hopped round and round the well in delight.

"The stinky ink is down the well. You can't stop Grizelda's spell!" he chanted.

With a great "KWARK!" he took off and flew away, bumping into tree branches as he went.

 79

Grizelda might think she's beaten

"What are we going to do?" asked
Charlotte, a tear trickling down her furry
cheek.

"Grizelda might think she's beaten
us," said Lily, giving the little puppy a
comforting hug, "but we're going to find
a way to get the ink."

"We need another
bucket," said Goldie.

"And some more
rope," said Jess.

"I know!" cried
Charlotte, wiping
her eyes. "We'll

use my flask as a bucket." She unclipped her pink flask from her collar. Then she unscrewed the lid and tipped out her lunchtime drink.

"That will be perfect!" declared Jess. "What a clever idea."

Then Lily ran into the tangle of undergrowth and came back with a long vine. "We can use this as a rope!"

"That's great, Lily!" said Goldie.

She tied it firmly to Charlotte's flask and Jess lowered it into the well.

"It's reached the ink!" she said after a moment. "I can feel the flask is heavier!"

She pulled on the vine.

At last the flask appeared at the top of the well, brimming with deep blue ink that twinkled in the sunlight. They grinned at each other in delight.

"We've done it!" said Jess.

"Thanks to you and your good

idea, Charlotte," said Goldie.

Wagging her tail excitedly, Charlotte took the flask in her paws and quickly screwed the lid on. She hooked it back on to her collar.

Scrambling under the overgrown weeds and roots, they were soon back at Spelltop School. But when they got there they stopped in disbelief.

There was no sign of the little school with its thatched roof and beautiful flowers. Instead, every building was covered in Grizelda's evil vines. The library had almost disappeared under a

tangle of creepers.

"We have to get the ink to Professor Wiggly straight away," said Jess.

"But where's the door?" said Goldie in alarm.

They ran to the library and tried to tug the creepers aside. Lily felt as if she was pulling open heavy curtains. She had to heave them hard to get them to move, but she could only just pull them back enough to touch the door. She felt around for the handle and at last her fingers found it. It took all her strength to turn it and push the door open.

It was dark inside the library. The vines outside had covered the windows, only letting a faint green light through the glass.

"Professor Wiggly, where are you?" called Lily, worried.

"I'm here!" came a voice. Jess and Lily looked around for the bookworm. They found him sitting at his desk. He had

 85

his blue feathered quill and *Perfect Plant Potions* ready in front of him. The weeds were still creeping out of the book and trailing round the desk.

"We've got the ink!" said Charlotte, running over with her flask.

"I knew I could count on you," exclaimed the professor. He picked up his empty ink bottle and took off the silver lid. "Pour it in and we'll get going!"

Lily held the ink bottle while Jess carefully poured the ink inside. It twinkled like a calm sea as it trickled in. The bottle was soon full of the magical blue liquid.

 86

Professor Wriggly stirred it with his quill

until a puff of smoke came out of the pot.

"There," he said. "That's done it."

But then the

door opened.

"Kwark!"

Everyone

turned to

see Cosmo

flapping in. He

flew straight

on to Professor

Wiggly's table.

"You

thought you'd beat Grizelda, did you?" he squawked. "Well, you won't. Your magic only keeps witches out of the library. It doesn't stop flamingos!" He flew round the room, knocking books off the shelves. "Books are stupid and boring!"

"Oh, no!" groaned Lily. "How is Professor Wiggly going to write the spells out again with Cosmo around?"

She stared at Jess and Goldie. They were looking as worried as she was.

But Charlotte was smiling. "I've got an idea," she said.

CHAPTER EIGHT

A Brilliant Idea

"Cosmo!" Charlotte called loudly.

Cosmo gave a squawk of surprise.

"What do you want?" he said rudely.

"I can help you to fly without crashing," said Charlotte.

Cosmo thrust his long beak close

to Charlotte's face and peered at her.
"How?" he demanded. "You're not a
flamingo. You don't even have wings."

But Charlotte didn't back away. "I'm
sure I can find a book that will tell you
all about flying straight," she said.

Cosmo's beak dropped open in
amazement. "Really?" he squawked.

"Of course," said Charlotte. "Books are
a great way to learn things."

"Charlotte's quite right," said Professor
Wiggly, beaming. He handed her the
golden bookmark. "Use this and you'll
find the perfect book."

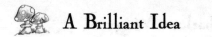

Charlotte's tail wagged in excitement as she waved the bookmark in circles. One of the books on a nearby shelf began to jostle the others. Then it burst from its place and floated down into her paws. She searched through it for the right page, then she showed it to Cosmo.

Cosmo stuck his beak into the book, mouthing the words as he read. "I must

use my tail feathers!" he declared. "Up, down, left, right."

Frowning with concentration, he launched himself into the air and swooped around the room. Lily and Jess could see his tail moving up, down, left and right. He landed without falling over.

"Kwark!" he screeched in delight. "I did it! Books aren't stupid after all!"

Charlotte gave Cosmo a big smile. Cosmo shuffled his feet and looked at the floor. "I'm sorry I helped Grizelda," he muttered. "I'm sorry I tried to hurt the books. I didn't know they were so useful."

 92

"Would you like to
learn more about
flying?" asked
Charlotte.
Cosmo's
eyes lit up. "Yes please!" he squawked.

"Then why not borrow this book?"
Professor Wiggly took the book stamp
and stamped the front page. "You can
take it away with you," he told the
flamingo. "Just remember to bring it back
in two weeks."

"I will!" Cosmo exclaimed. "I promise."
He looked at the shelves heaving with

books. "And then can I borrow another one?"

"Of course you can, my boy," said Professor Wiggly. He handed Cosmo a bright pink card. "This is your own special library card. Bring it when you come back. We'll be delighted to see you."

Cosmo was so excited he tried to turn a somersault. He picked himself up from the floor, grasped the book with one foot and hopped towards the door.

"Thank you," he squawked.

He took off. As he flew away, they could hear him muttering under his

A Brilliant Idea

breath. "Up, down, left, right."

Lily and Jess ran over and gave
Charlotte a big kiss.

"Well done, Charlotte," added Professor
Wiggly.

"I didn't do much," said the little pup
shyly. "I just know that there's a book for
everyone."

"Now we must get the potions put
right," said Goldie.

Jess wiped the spilled ink off the
desk and Lily filled the pot again from
Charlotte's flask. Professor Wiggly sat
at his desk, *Perfect Plant Potions* in front

of him. The quill danced in the air for a
moment, dipped into the ink and then
began to fly across the pages. It moved
so quickly it became a blur. The words of
the bad spells faded away and new ones
appeared in their place.

The quill stopped and floated down
to the desk. There was a flash of sparkly

light and the weeds disappeared from *Perfect Plant Potions*. Now they could see its glittery green cover with golden flowers again.

Light flooded in through the library windows as the creepers outside vanished.

Professor Wiggly rubbed his hands together happily. "That'll do the trick."

They all rushed out of the library. Grizelda's horrible vines and weeds were shrinking away from the school and the forest. Soon, they were tiny blobs of slime, then they vanished in wisps of nasty green smoke.

"The school's back to normal!" exclaimed Goldie.

"And the forest's even more beautiful than ever!" cried Lily.

There was a burst of cheering behind them and Professor Gogglewing and all the young pupils ran out to celebrate. The animals made a big ring and skipped round the girls, Goldie and Charlotte, singing in delight.

"How can we thank you?" said the headmaster. "You've saved our school – and Friendship Forest – from Grizelda."

Professor Cutiepaws came rushing

towards them. She burst into the ring, her blue eyes round with amazement. "You've got rid of that spell," she exclaimed. "However did you do it?"

"Clever Charlotte and her books," said Jess, proudly.

"Lily, Jess and Goldie helped too," said Charlotte, wagging her tail.

"Then you deserve a reward, Charlotte," said Professor Gogglewing.

"I know the very thing!" said Professor Wiggly. "I appoint you my library monitor." He handed Charlotte a big shiny badge with "Library Monitor" on it

in gold letters.

"Thank you!" The little puppy beamed with pride as she pinned it on to the strap of her flask.

"By my whiskers," Professor Cutiepaws said to the girls, "it must have been very difficult for you to stop such a clever plan."

"We'll always stop Grizelda!" declared Jess.

"We have to go now, Charlotte," said Lily. "Enjoy looking after those library books."

"And reading them!" declared

Charlotte, her eyes bright.

The girls knelt down and gave her a big hug goodbye then waved to Professor Gogglewing, Professor Wiggly, Professor Cutiepaws and all the pupils.

Goldie led the way to the Friendship Tree, past starflower bushes and pale pink roses, all filling the air with lovely scents. She tapped the trunk and the door appeared, golden light spilling out.

The girls stepped into the golden glow and found themselves back in Brightley Meadow.

"What an adventure," said Lily.

"Yes," said Jess. "But let's go back and check on those three little pups!"

The girls crossed Brightley Stream and stepped back into the pen in Lily's garden. Two of the pups were tumbling about on the grass, gently nipping at each other's ears. The third one was snuffling at Lily's library book. Lily picked up the book she'd been looking at earlier. "Look, it's opened on a picture of puppies just like these ones!" she exclaimed. "They're Puggles – a cross between a pug and a beagle."

"What a clever pup you are, finding the

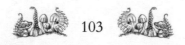

right page!" said Jess, stroking the puppy's head.

Lily and Jess smiled at each other. They knew another puppy who liked looking things up in books!

The End

Lily and Jess are having lots of fun at Spelltop School, where the animals of Friendship Forest learn all about magic. But something is making the school's enchantment go wonky – it must be the work of the wicked witch, Grizelda ...

Can tiny meerkat Layla Brighteye spot what's wrong and help the girls save the school?

Find out in the next Magic Animal Friends book,

Layla Brighteye Keeps a Lookout

Turn over for a sneak peek ...

"Look at Giggles go!" Jess Forester said to her best friend, Lily Hart. "He doesn't stay still for a moment, does he?"

Giggles the parrot was flying around an aviary, an enormous cage made of wire netting and wood. It was part of Helping Paw Wildlife Hospital, which Lily's parents ran inside the barn close by. Both girls adored helping to care for the poorly animals. As well as Giggles, the aviary contained a duck with a damaged wing, who was nibbling at some lettuce, and two young pigeons. They were cooing sleepily in the autumn sunshine, their heads gently resting together.

While Lily went into the aviary to fill up water bowls for the birds, Jess tried to paint Giggles. She had her paints and sketchbook spread out on the grass in front of her. Jess squirted some yellow and blue paint into a pot, and mixed them together with her paintbrush to make green. Giggles flashed by in a blur of green feathers. A white bandage was tied around his foot.

"He's going to be hard to paint, flying around like that," said Lily. "Are you going to paint his bandage too?"

Jess held up the paint pot, frowning. "I need to mix the right colour for his feathers first," she said. "This green doesn't look bright enough."

Giggles shot past again. "Bedtime!" he squawked. "Bedtime, Giggles!"

Lily grinned. "My dad said parrots copy what they hear people say. I bet his owner says 'Bedtime' to him every night!"

"Night, Giggles!" the parrot squawked. "Night, night!"

Both girls laughed.

"I love it when he talks," said Jess. "Do you know what it reminds me of?"

"Friendship Forest!" said Lily, with a trill of excitement.

Friendship Forest was a secret magical world where all the animals lived in little cottages, and visited the Toadstool Café for honey buns and hazelnut cream milkshakes. Best of all, they could talk!

Read

Layla Brighteye Keeps a Lookout

to find out what happens next!

Jess and Lily's Animal Facts

Lily and Jess love lots of different animals –
both in Friendship Forest
and in the real world.

Here are their top facts about

PUPPIES

like Charlotte Waggytail:

- Dogs and humans have such a strong bond they are sometimes called "man's best friend"

- Some dogs enter competitions such as agility and obedience games, racing and pulling sledges

- Dog can hear sounds four times further away than humans can

- Pet dogs are omnivores, which means they eat vegetables and meats

- Dogs are not colour blind – this is a myth! They can actually see in colour, but not as brightly as humans

Can you keep the secret?

There's lots of fun for everyone at
www.magicanimalfriends.com

Play games and explore the secret world of
Friendship Forest, where animals can talk!

Join the
Magic Animal Friends Club!

✳ Special competitions ✳

✳ Exclusive content ✳

✳ All the latest Magic Animal Friends news! ✳

To join the Club, simply go to

www.magicanimalfriends.com/join-our-club/